The Little Green Hippopotamus

by Charles Hutson

This book is a work of fiction. Names, characters, places, and incidents are either a product of the author's imagination or are use fictitiously. Any resemblance to any persons, or hippos living or dead, or to the actual events or locales is purely coincidental. However, this author makes no assurances that hippos, green or gray or whatever, are not real and do not have little stories like this in their day to day lives.

This book is licensed for your personal enjoyment and should not be re-sold or given away to others except as a purchased gift. The author has put a lot of hard work into the creation of this book. If you respect the right of the author to earn an income from his efforts, I would ask that you consider purchasing your own copy. Thanks for your consideration.

Copyright 2014 Charles R. Hutson. All rights reserved including the right to reproduce this book or portions thereof in any form without the express written permission of the author, except for lines or quotes used in connection with reviews.

Contents

Chapter One---Shades of Gray

Chapter Two---Breakfast for Three

Chapter Three---Thunder and Lightning

Chapter Four---A Plan

Chapter Five---Hungry Hungry Hippo

Chapter Six---Brown Bottles

Chapter Seven---The Silence of the Hippos

Chapter Eight---Prison Break

Chapter Nine---Up The River

Chapter Ten---The Rock

Chapter Eleven---Ring Around the...Avocado?

Chapter Twelve---Ava Disappears

Chapter Thirteen---A Funeral March

Chapter Fourteen---A Green Ghost

Chapter Fifteen---Final Destination

Chapter One—Shades of Gray

When Hortense Hippopotamus was born, no one ever really expected her to STAY green. Though none of the hippopotami had ever seen a green birth color before, they all assumed it was a just that, another birth color, like the usual pink that hippos are born. In the same way that some human babies appear bluish, or purplish, or even yellowish at birth, the hippos all thought that Hortense would grow out of it so no hippo thought too much about it to begin with. But as the hours grew into days, and the days into weeks, and finally into months, it began to look more and more like this little hippo was going to stay green forever. As a matter of fact, her parents, who had already given her the name of Hortense after her mother's grandmother, decided...because her skin was such a beautiful avocado green, to rename her Avocado...Ava for short.

Now, Hortense...er...Avocado's parents were of course shades of gray, as are most hippos. Harris Hippo, Ava's father, was a dark gray...almost black. And Hilda Hippo, her mother, was a light gray...with just a hint of tan. All of Ava's grandparents and great grandparents and so on as far back as they could remember, were all...various shades of gray. And when the entire hippo herd got together to talk about it, none of them had ever heard of a green hippopotamus. Occasionally, there were shades of brown, and even a total black color, or even a white albino color would pop up in some hippo groups, and that was well-known and accepted...but no hippo had ever heard, anytime or anywhere, of a green hippopotamus. There was no reason at all that anyone could think of for Avocado to be green...but there she was...as green as you please.

Well, you can imagine what kind of effect Avocado's greenness had on the other hippos. Because she was green, she was viewed as very different from all the others. At first, the other hippos tried to ignore the difference with the hope that maybe one day it would just go away. But, as the months passed, it became more and more clear to all, that Avocado was green to stay.

For a while after that, the other hippos were...polite...but they always eyed Avocado suspiciously. They weren't quite sure what to make of a green hippopotamus. They began to talk in whispers behind the backs of Harris and Hilda and Ava. One of the worst gossipers was a big, boring, blowhard hippo named Harold. Harold had always been very opinionated about everything, most of the time without logic or reason. He liked to figuratively, throw his weight around. If he had been a child, he would have been called a bully. As an adult, they just called him pushy and obnoxious...but unfortunately, some hippos still listened to what he had to say.

When some of the lady hippos were talking one day to Harold's wife, Henrietta, she asked the question, "What do you suppose is WRONG with that poor little hippo? I wonder what could have happened to make her green."

Harold was only too happy to put in his two cents worth. "Well," he jumped in, "I'll tell you what I think! I think it's some kind of weird disease. If I were you, I'd keep my kids away from her or before you know it, they'll ALL be turning green...and then who knows what could happen! I know we're not going to let OUR son Herman play with her anymore. Who knows what kind of strange disease it is?"

The hippos talked and talked about it that day and they got to thinking of all the terrible things that could ever happen to any hippo...and they imagined that being green was the cause of it all. They let themselves get totally carried away. And thanks to Harold, they began to make their own children stay as far away from Avocado as possible.

That was too bad too, because Avocado was one of the sweetest and smartest little hippos that anyone would ever hope to meet. She was always friendly and polite, and she never got into mischief...well, no major mischief like some of the others. And she was especially cute.

When she first learned to talk she couldn't quite pronounce her name. It always came out "Ah-du-ca-du..." Her parents of course, as parents tend to do, told the cute little tale to every hippo in the herd. They didn't quite realize at the time that they were slowly being banished from the daily get-togethers. At first, it was just a few who wandered away when they came around. Then gradually, it became obvious that every hippo began to leave when they even got close to the group.

Meanwhile, the same thing was happening to Avocado. Though the other hippo kids had never had a problem with Ava's color, they began to pick up on what their parents were saying. Where they used to think that Avocado's color was pretty neat, after listening to their parents for a while they began to get scared. A few of the young hippos, especially a budding bully named Herman(Harold's son by the way)began to make up mean stories about Ava. He would tell the others to not get too close to Avocado or they would TURN GREEN AND DIE!

Kids can be cruel...but it is a learned trait.

Sooner or later, one by one, ALL of the other hippo parents were warning their children "Don't play with that Avocado or you'll be catching god knows what!" Or "Stay away from her, you don't know what she has!" Or even "Watch out for Avocado! That green might rub off and poison you!"

Can you imagine any responsible adult saying such a thing? But they did. The children had to learn it from somewhere.

And one by one, Avocado's little "friends" stopped playing with her. At first they made excuses. They had to go home for supper...or they promised their parents they would do some chores, or whatever...just to get away from her! Their parents had them worried beyond reason. They even began to fear Avocado so much that going home to do chores was PREFERABLE to playing with her!

All the while, Avocado was just as sweet as ever. She tried not to let it bother her. And she wasn't the least bit mean back to them, but she did feel hurt. She didn't understand. She hadn't changed a bit, but now no one wanted to play with her. She was still the same nice little hippo she had always been. Nothing had changed...yet she soon realized that no hippo wanted to be around her anymore...simply because she was GREEN.

One evening Ava came home crying. "Mommy," she sobbed, "why won't anyone play with me anymore? What's the matter with me? Why do I have to be green?"

A tear came to Hilda Hippo's eye, then more as she struggled to find an answer. She lay her big chin on Avocado's forehead and opened her mouth to speak...but nothing came out. She tried to soothe Avocado even though her own heart was breaking.

Every parent hopes and dreams that their child will be able to make it in life without being tormented and taunted by others for being some kind of different. Too tall, too short, red hair, freckles, glasses, birthmarks, too fat, too thin, too slow, or even too smart. At some time or other, children, and even grownups, have been taunted by others...just for being a little different than them.

It's a cruel fact of life she told Avocado that evening, that as long as there are differences, there will always be some who will be frightened by the differences. And in order to try to hide their fear, they will try to hurt or humiliate or make fun of those who are different. The problem she told Ava, is not in the one who is different, but in the ones who taunt and tease them.

She was right of course, but that didn't really make Avocado feel any better. They both knew it was all so true, but they cried together just the same.

Chapter Two—Breakfast for Three

The days passed and Avocado grew mostly oblivious to their remarks. She was a tough little hippo and she didn't give up easily. Many times she tried to join in with the others, but when she did the games always seemed to break up quickly. Most of the little hippos snuck away without even acknowledging Ava, but there were a few who still made lame excuses about why they had to go. Little Heidi Hippo was one of them. She was the smallest hippo in the herd and she always looked as if she felt as bad as Avocado. She was always the last one to stumble away mumbling excuses. Ava felt sad for Heidi, but she felt even sadder for herself. Though she tried not to cry, sometimes she just couldn't help herself. She felt so all alone...

Not only was Ava an outcast, but at the same time that she was being pushed away by the little hippos, her parents were also feeling the cold shoulder from the adult hippos. They were no longer welcome at the grown up hippo functions. It used to be that each morning before the young hippos were awake, all of the adults would get up early and gather down in the jungle clearing for a quiet breakfast of tender grasses coated with the fresh morning dew. And as the morning passed, one by one the little ones would wake up and begin to form their own little cluster close to, but a little off to the side of the parents. While the older hippos spent their time grazing and keeping a watchful eye on their youngsters, the little hippos were alive with the morning energy of children. They would spend more of their time playing than eating. They did grab a bite here and there, but eating wasn't their priority. They knew there would always be time to eat later. Besides, their little bodies didn't require nearly as much fuel as did the adults.

A similar scene used to play out each evening. After a long day of grazing in the hot sun, all of the hippopotami would stroll down to the river where they would wash off the dusty day and drink their fill of water. The adults would soak and socialize, while the children did more laughing and playing along the edge of the river. At least that's how it used to be.

Now things were different. Instead of just two separate groups, one for the adults and one for the children...now there were three. The third was a forlorn little gathering made up of Harris and Hilda...and Avocado...which worked out fine for the main herd...as long as they didn't wander too close. "Wouldn't want to catch something, you know," reminded Harold Hippo at times.

And so, it continued that way, day after endless day...until one day...

Chapter Three—Thunder and Lightening

The day began like any other. The main pod of adult hippos had awakened early and were munching their morning meal in the clearing. And of course, off to one side, were Harris and Hilda. Avocado was still not awake, nor were the other little hippos. If it were not for the distance between Ava's parents and the main herd, one might think it was just like the days before the Avocado scare began. As the young hippos had not arrived on the scene yet, all was still peaceful and serene. It seemed like the start of any other beautiful day. None of them could have imagined what was about to happen.

Back behind the tree line just out of earshot of the hippo herd, a ring of hunters waited for the signal. They had set a trap for the hippos at the far end of the clearing. The hungry hippopotami stood chomping peacefully...blissfully unaware of the danger!

Then, like a sudden flash of lightning accompanied by cracks of thunder, the hunters seemed to burst out of everywhere with wild yells and guns blazing! The poor frightened hippos didn't have any idea of what to do except to try to get away from these terrible, noisy two-legged creatures. There was only one direction they could go...but of course, that was the plan.

Through a small opening at one end of the clearing, the terrified hippos raced to what they thought would be their freedom...but no sooner had they each one passed through the opening...they realized that there was no way out! And with the other hippos close behind them, there wasn't even a chance to warn them. It was only as the gate closed behind the last two hippos, Harris and Hilda, that they all understood. The hunters had built a strong corral of logs and ropes. They were all trapped together!

Oh, those hippos bellowed! They let out their wildest and angriest hippo hollers...but the hunters were not the least bit scared. Instead they were all talking and laughing and patting each other on the backs. They were very pleased with what they had done. The hippos bellowed even more but the hunters didn't seem to be afraid. They all just went on to doing other things.

"O.K. Great job!" said one man who appeared to be their leader. "Now let's get them on the trucks before they figure out how to get out of there."

"Get out of here? What do they mean, get out of here," said Harris Hippo, "I don't see any way out," he muttered as he looked thoroughly around the corral. He was right, but he was wrong too. The cage did have them totally enclosed, but it was a relatively flimsy cage by hippo standards, built just to keep them in for a brief time.

Alas, hippos have always been slow thinking animals. Not dumb, just slow. Given enough time, they would have realized that they could have pushed the fencing down with just a little extra effort together. But as it was, they were much too frightened and nervous. And when hippos are upset, they take even longer to understand.

The hunters on the other hand, knew exactly what they were doing. If they were going to keep their catch, they would have to transfer them to their stronger central cage quickly before the hippos had time to calm down and think. While two men with guns remained to guard the corral, the rest of the men went back for the trucks. It wasn't long before the first truck was backed up to the gate and began loading hippos up the ramp. The man who gave the orders, his name was Johnson, spoke again as he watched the loading. "This is a nice bunch of hippos here. We ought to make a bundle selling them to the zoos."

All this, while in some thick underbrush just off the clearing, a small group of young hippos watched in horror. They weren't sure exactly what was happening, but they knew something was terribly wrong by the bellowing of their parents. They had been awakened from their slumber when the first of the shooting and hollering began. Now they stood silent, almost in shock, as they watched their parents being loaded onto these strange wheeled machines. Avocado, who had slept with her parents away from the others as usual, was the last to arrive. As she approached the group of little hippos, she saw what was happening. She quickly forgot about being an outcast.

"What's going on?" she asked quietly.

"Aaaaah!" jumped Herman Hippo. "It's Avocado! Let's get out of here!" Herman, though he was the son of Harold Hippo, was not REALLY that much like Harold, but his father wanted Herman to be like him, so he bullied Herman just like he did everyone else. But Herman was more confused than anything. Still, it was true to his upbringing that he was the only one to worry about Avocado in spite of the grave situation in front of them.

Had the other little hippos not been too stunned to move, and so, too solid a wall to allow Herman to pass through, Herman might have run out into the clearing, exposing their presence to the hunters and possibly causing their capture. This was one time that being slow really saved them.

And it was the last straw for Avocado! Up until now, she had taken it all in stride, without losing her temper, and without fighting back. Through all the trials of dealing with their prejudice, she somehow seemed to have matured more than the others, and she had always been much smarter than them.

"Now, listen!" she barked softly yet firmly, "I've had enough of this stupid nonsense! We've played together all our lives until somebody got a stupid idea that I'm some kind of poison! Has anything EVER happened to you because of me? NO! Don't you understand that there is nothing different with me except my color? Can't you see how ridiculous it is for you to run away from me JUST BECAUSE I'M GREEN?" She paused as if waiting for someone to answer her questions, but never waited long enough for them to actually do it.

She went on. "For just once in your lives, stop and think! Don't you see what's happening? They're taking our parents away! Listen to me! Someone's got to do something, and we're the only ones who can! We've got to figure out a way to help them, and to do that, we've got to work together!"

The little hippos stood back with wide eyes and

open mouths at Avocado's outburst. Ava had never so much as uttered one harsh word before, but now she was really letting them have it. And somehow they knew she was right about all of it. They HAD to do something...and they realized that playing 'stay away from Avocado' was not going to help anything. They may have had some stupid ideas, but they weren't stupid!

A small voice piped up from the back of the group. "What ARE we going to do, Ava?" It was little Heidi Hippo. Avocado smiled. Of course Heidi would be the first one to speak up. But before Avocado could say anything, the trucks began to pull away with their loads of hippos. She spoke quickly and surely. "I don't know yet," she said, "but I do know that we've got to follow those machines. Let's go!" she ordered. "And keep out of sight. We mustn't let them see us."

She needn't have worried about that. The hunters were so pleased with themselves and so sure of their load that they never even bothered to look back. If they had, they would have seen a forlorn looking bunch of determined little hippos out to save their world. Already they were huffing and puffing from pumping their short little stumps of legs much faster than they were ever designed to go. Though the big trucks were only plodding along over the rough jungle terrain, even that pace was almost too much for the little band. The smaller hippos were already lagging far behind, and even the frontrunners were quickly losing ground on the trucks. If the trip had been much longer, the little hippos would have been lost.

Luckily, the hunters' main camp was not too far away. It was just far enough from the grazing grounds that the hippos had not heard the hunters building the

BIG cage. If the hippos were still back at home now, they would not have heard the loud engines of the trucks as they shifted gears and strained under their heavy loads to back up to the big corral. They would not have heard the slamming and crashing of the truck gates as they took turns unloading their catch. They wouldn't even have heard the exuberant cheers of the hunters as they finished their day's labors and began celebration of their successful hunt. They wouldn't have heard any of it...if they were still at home...

Chapter Four---A Plan

When the little hippos got close enough to the camp to see what was happening, they found their parents had been placed in a smaller but much stronger looking, cage-like structure made from even larger logs and held together even more securely by huge cords of rope. The hunters knew what they were doing when they prepared this cage. The corral was a veritable fortress even to the full group of adult hippos. Even if the pod had been able to run at full hippopotamus speed and smash into the sides, the corral was not likely to give way. But that didn't matter because there was no way they could have gotten up to full speed inside the cage. There was barely enough room for them to move around. The hippopotamus prison had been well thought out.

"Oh, no!" whined Herman Hippo when he saw the cage. We'll never be able to get them out of there!" The others too, saw the desperation of their mission. Some sobbed, and the rest fell into a stunned silence.

Avocado was discouraged too. She had no ideas before how they might have been able to help the adults, but now, the situation seemed even more hopeless. Not only was the cage strong, but it was located in such a way that it was visible from all angles by the men in their camp. What she saw discouraged her very much, but she wasn't ready to give up. Instead of letting desperation take hold of her as it had the others, she began to look more closely, as if to convince herself that there was really a chance. She whispered to herself to reinforce that thought. "There's got to be a way! There's got to be a way! Now think Ava, we've got to help them!"

The others didn't even notice when Avocado slipped away to get a closer look at the camp. She watched in awe as the last truck backed up and unloaded the last few hippos. She watched disheartened as the heavy gate swung shut. She watched silently as the man moved the log that latched the gate into place. For a moment as she watched the man struggle with the heavy log latch, she felt the desperation her little group had felt a few minutes earlier. Then suddenly it hit her. The seed of a plan sprang into her mind!

The log latch was made with handles sticking out from the front side so that the hunters could grasp it more easily to make the log move. The log itself was greased with something that made it slide more easily for the men. And though the log was heavy for a man…it was not that much for a hippopotamus!

She had seen the adult hippos toss around such logs like toothpicks. And even the young hippos had many times moved similar sized logs with relative ease as they played their games. What was a struggle for a man, would be easy even for the smaller hippos…if they could get the men away from the area long enough to get the job done. Though the cage was not guarded closely, the main camp sat where anyone looking that direction would have full view of the hippo corral.

Avocado was a little frustrated seeing that there was nothing at all they could do for the moment, but now she had hope. She went back to the others to report her findings. "Perhaps we can get to the gate after dark," she told them. "For now, all we can do is wait.

Chapter Five---Hungry, Hungry Hippo

The sun rose to its highest point and then began its journey down the other side of the sky. All day long the little hippos patiently took turns standing watch where they could see the corral. The rest of the group stationed themselves a little further away from the campsite.

In all the excitement of the morning, the little hippos realized they had forgotten about their morning feeding. But now, the lack of food was beginning to tell. It was while Herman was on watch with Avocado that it finally hit him. As he would on any normal day he reached down to grab a mouthful of whatever was closest to him. Today it was a tender looking little bush off to his right.

Avocado was alert for even the smallest movement, and realized immediately what he was going to do. "STOP!" she whispered sharply.

Poor Herman was so startled that he stopped in mid chomp. Though he had been the biggest bully of the group and the one who was the meanest to Avocado, he had quickly learned to respect her authority.

"Wh—What's wrong?" he whispered back to her. He stood frozen with fear as if a lion were about to plunge at him for the kill. Actually it wasn't quite that bad, but it could have been terrible. As you can imagine, if you ever stopped to think about it...hippos....even little ones, make a LOT of noise when they eat. With all their yanking and tearing at brush and grasses and branches, and all that chomping and grinding and growling as they chew the food with their rather large mouths, they can make quite a racket when they dine. If Herman had been allowed to complete his exceptionally large, and especially hungry bite, the hunters would have no doubt heard the sounds and come over to investigate.

"I know you're hungry Herman, I was beginning to notice that myself, but we'd better wait until we get back to the others," she explained, "or they might hear us."

"Whew!" gasped Herman looking a little sheepish. "You're right. I wasn't thinking." He smiled at her a big hippo smile. "Thanks," he added.

With that, the two little hippos redirected themselves to the job at hand realizing that somehow they shared a bond that went beyond the color of their skin. It was only now in this time of crisis that the bond had become visible to them. Avocado looked again at Herman. He was still smiling at her. She smiled back.

Chapter Six---Brown Bottles

It was almost dark when it was Avocado's turn to stand watch again. The hunters who had been occupied with various work tasks throughout the day, were beginning to settle down for the evening. One by one they gathered by the campfire, but only after they each stopped at one of the trucks and pulled out some curious brown bottles from which they took long drinks.

At first they just carried on conversations about all kinds of things that Avocado knew nothing about, then as she watched, their conversations became louder and more heated. Their quiet talk at the beginning had turned into loud, boisterous, and sometimes angry sounding arguments. Two of them got into a fight, but Johnson broke it up.

After that, one of the men got up and touched a black box which made music play. They had heard music before from some of the natives who lived in the jungle, but no music like this, and all from within a little black box. Ava was intrigued with the humans. Some of the hunters now got up and danced. Ava had seen the natives dance before also, but this was very different from their dances. Between the music and the dancing, the arguing stopped. Now all the men were laughing and joking again. They laughed and carried on so that when it was time for Avocado's shift to end, she wanted to stay on to see just exactly what was going on. She wanted to know all about these strange human rituals.

Avocado watched closely, trying to understand it

all, and more importantly, what it meant to the hippos if anything. But after a time, almost as suddenly as they began their strange behavior, an even stranger thing happened. One of the men who had stopped dancing earlier and sat down by the campfire, suddenly fell over, looking quite dead! The other men began laughing. Avocado watched with wide-eyed amazement.

"He's plastered!" said one and they laughed some more. Avocado didn't quite know what "plastered" meant but it was surely another word for dead she thought. He lay on the ground still clutching one of the brown bottles in his hand.

Johnson laughed too. Then he added. "You guys need to wrap it up anyway. We've got a long trip tomorrow and we all need to be fresh. Throw Jonesy in his tent and let's wind it up for the evening. Abernathy, you go out and check on the hippos. Make sure they're secure for the night. Wouldn't want anything to happen to our paychecks now, would we?"

The men grumbled as they stumbled over to pick up the dead looking man. Some of them took last drinks from their brown bottles and threw them into the fire with a loud breaking sound. Ava was watching the scene so intently and thinking so seriously that the noise startled her. The man was talking about a long trip tomorrow. She understood that they intended to take the adult hippos with them. She also knew that whatever the little hippos were going to do, they had to do it tonight...or they would never get another chance!

Even as she thought, the hunter's camp was beginning to quiet down. One of the men touched the black box again and the music stopped. One by one the men finished their evening chores and disappeared into their tents. Soon the camp was so quiet that the only sounds she could hear were the night sounds of the jungle. The fire burned low until just the coals were visible, glowing a dim orange. There was nothing else to see, but Avocado watched a little longer before she decided it was time to go.

Now she moved quickly back to the place where her little group was stationed. They were all exhausted from a hard, tiring and stressful day, Avocado moreso than any of them. While most of them had slept a fitful couple of hours, Ava had remained awake and alert most of the day and evening working on a plan. She realized there was a chance it wouldn't work, and they would only get one chance, but what other choice was there?

She explained her plan to the little hippos. A first group would consist only of her and Herman. He was the biggest and strongest of all the little hippos. He had always been boastful of his strength, and sometime bullied many of the smaller hippos including her, but now his strength would be the key to whole plan. Avocado hadn't particularly liked him, but he was the one she thought of when it came to moving the latch. If he couldn't do it, none of them could. He solemnly accepted his task.

The second group had only to wait at a designated spot near the edge of the hunter's camp. They would lead the adults away after the gate was opened…if it were opened.

It was the third group that would have what Avocado told them could be the most dangerous part of the plan. Avocado looked around at the faces of her playmates. All of them were only children. She hesitated, but she knew that the plan could totally fail for everyone unless they had a backup. Someone had to be ready in case something went wrong at the corral. They would need a diversion to give them a little more time…maybe enough time to complete the job of freeing the adults. If they didn't have this group, not only might they fail to get their parents out, but they could all end up trapped as well!

If the hunters were aroused for any reason, the third group had to run fast through the camp, and make a lot of noise! It would be their job to create a diversion to draw attention away from what was really happening at the corral. These hippos would have to go right into the camp as close to the humans as possible, and make them forget that there even was a cage full of hippos at all. There was the possibility she explained, that those in the third group could be captured, or even hurt in the confusion! She would make no assignments for this group, only take volunteers.

Chapter Seven---The Silence of the Hippos

It was quiet for a moment that seemed to last for hours. None of them said a word, nor did they look at each other. All of them were frightened, understandably so. Up until now, the worst any of them had ever to deal with was whether or not Avocado would really make them turn green and die. And they all knew deep inside them that it wasn't going to happen. Not really. It was just a matter of pressure from their parents and from their peers to conform to the standard…which said that Avocado was different and should be avoided. For that moment, it seemed like not one of them would volunteer for this part of the plan, but then from the back of the group in her tiny little hippo voice, the smallest and shyest little hippo of all spoke up.

"I'll go," said Heidi simply.

Avocado smiled sadly. As much as she wanted to tell Heidi that it wouldn't be necessary, that it wouldn't have to be her, she knew it had to be someone if they had an honest chance at freeing their parents. They could of course try it without the diversion group, but if anything went wrong, it was more than likely that almost all of them would end up being captured without exception. She nodded her head in acceptance of Heidi's offer.

"Anyone else?" she asked just the slightest bit annoyed. She realized that the tension and frustration were getting to her. "Anyone else?" she repeated more calmly.

"I'll go," said wimpy Hamilton Hippo. That was a big surprise. She had expected just about anyone but Hamilton. He had always seemed shy and scared about everything, the opposite end of the extreme from Herman, but he was also a little sweet on Heidi. Avocado had seen it, but Heidi never even noticed. Maybe this was just the thing to bring out his bravery...or his foolishness. But there was something else. She felt a certain closeness to Heidi when she volunteered. And now she felt that for Hamilton as well. Something seemed to be happening to all of them, and somehow it seemed only natural that all of them should rise to the occasion. She felt it even stronger as three more little hippos, Herbert, Hannah, and Haldon volunteered in quick succession to join Heidi and Hamilton. They were scared, sure. But they all realized that this was not a game. That this was for real...and for keeps!

"That's enough," said Avocado. "That's all we need." Too many and they would run more risk of being discovered before it was time. Too few, and there probably wouldn't be enough of them to create a proper diversion. They were ready now.

Avocado gave out the last of the directions. Heidi's group would go to the other side of the camp and find a place to wait...as close to the tents as they could get. Once they had plenty of time to get set, Ava and Herman would head for the prison that held all of their parents.

"Now remember," said Avocado to Heidi as she prepared to leave. "Don't take any chances! If everything goes well, just stay put. Give us plenty of time to get everyone away from there, and then come as quickly as you can to the meeting place. You only need to make a diversion IF the hunters wake up."

"Good luck!" she added as they turned to walk away.

Not one little hippo said any more as Heidi and her group disappeared into the darkness. No one spoke as they allowed time for Heidi and the others to get into their position. The silence of the hippos in the dark night was broken only when Ava gave the final signal. "Let's go," she said to Herman as the final group also headed for their position. She glanced back once at that group going off their way, then they too were swallowed up by the night.

Chapter Eight—Prison Break

The adult hippos looked bedraggled and forlorn in the dim moonlight. Or maybe it was just the bars framing them that made them look so pitiful. They were sleeping when Ava and Herman reached the cage.

"Pssst..." whispered Avocado. "Pssst...Hello!" It was Ava's father who heard her first.

"Avocado? Is that you?" Harris Hippo asked worriedly. "My goodness child, what are you doing here? We thought you were all safe back at home. You've got to get away from here before they catch you too!"

"No!" Avocado said firmly. "We've come to get you out of here," she added matter of factly.

"Harrumph...what's going on here?" snorted Harold Hippo indignantly. He had awakened when he heard the talking. Now he was fully awake and back to his obnoxious self. "How are YOU kids going to get us out of here?" he asked scornfully. "Even with all of us together, we can't break open this prison! What do you think YOU'RE going to be able to do?" He hadn't even noticed that his own son stood there with her.

Harold had always been the most obnoxious hippopotamus in the whole pod, and Harris had never especially liked him, but this time he had to agree with Harold. "He's right, Ava. There's nothing you can do," he said sadly. "It's better that you and Herman and whoever else came with you, go on back home. Get as far away as you can! The only thing worse than never seeing you again would be to see you children captured also."

But Avocado was not to be discouraged. "Sorry Dad. Can't do it," she said. "We're here now and we're not going to give up without at least trying." She directed her attention to Herman and the gate. "O.K., Herman. Let's see what we can do."

With that, Ava and Herman set about deciding how to get the best grip on the log latch. It was obvious that there wasn't enough space for both of them to work the latch. And it looked a LOT bigger than Avocado had first thought when she saw it from a distance. She wasn't so sure now if Herman WOULD be able to move it or not!

Herman grasped the handle with his strong young hippo mouth and began to push with all his might! He pushed and he pushed. All of the adult hippos inside the corral were awake now and they saw what Herman was trying to do. They all held their breaths and groaned along with Herman. If the power of positive thinking would work from behind bars that log latch would have went flying, because every single one of them were gritting their teeth and pushing right alongside him in their minds. They all gasped for breath when he stopped to take a break.

"I think I felt it move a little," Herman said with continued enthusiasm. Avocado wasn't so sure. As a matter of fact, she was pretty sure it DIDN'T move at all. She was feeling very desperate. She had been so sure that they could do it that she hadn't thought of any other plan...or even if there were any other plan to think of. She was quiet as Herman began to push again.

"The END of the log, Avocado!" It was Harris Hippo speaking excitedly. "The end of the log …" he repeated. "Push on the end of the log while Herman uses the handle…" She looked at him oddly and then at the log.

Of course! That was the one place she could help! She looked at her father and nodded an acknowledgment of understanding, and then again at Herman who had stopped pushing when he heard them talking. She explained to him, and set herself in place.

"O.K., Herman. I'm ready. Let's try it now!" she said. She dropped her head and butted it against the end of the log. "One…two…three!" she whispered loudly and they both began pushing with everything they had.

The log responded!

"It's moving!" gasped Hilda Hippo from inside the cage. Indeed it was moving! It moved so smoothly and quickly that it didn't stop when it reached the end of its track! It moved right on past the edge of the gate and fell to the ground with a loud "CRASH!" The hippos all froze hoping that it hadn't been as loud as they imagined.

Their hopes were not realized. One of the men HAD heard it. He groggily emerged from the tent in his long johns to look around. "What's going on out there?" he hollered. "Is there anybody out there?" he shouted again into the darkness. No one answered. He ducked back in to the tent and came out with a flashlight. It would only be a matter of seconds before someone else heard the commotion, and only seconds more before they would think to check the corral.

With splendid timing, there came Heidi and her small band of renegade hippos, snorting and whooping and bellowing like it was the end of the world. Even from the corral, the adults could see the hunter's eyes grow wide with surprise as the wild gang of mini-hippos bore down on him. He screamed like a little girl and dove out of the way to avoid being trampled by this would-be stampede of tiny hippos.

"Wake up Mates!" he shouted. "We've got wild baby hippos everywhere!"

It would have been an amusing sight to see Heidi and her group tearing up the hunters camp like demented rats were it not a matter of life and death for the hippos. Avocado reminded the adults of their mission.

"Come On! We've got to get out of here…NOW!" And with that, the adults pushed open the gate and quickly filed out with Herman in the lead running his little stump legs as fast as they could move.

Chapter Nine—Up The River

As planned, they all met together just away from the camp area. Together they headed to the designated meeting place to wait for the diversion group to return. Because it was so dark, they knew that the hunters would not be able to track them effectively until morning. They felt reasonably safe and happy as they waited.

One by one the others returned. There was joy in Avocado's heart as she counted them down. A successful plan...and all of them returning safely. Hamilton, Hannah, Haldon, Herbert...except...where's Heidi?

"Where's Heidi?" she repeated her thought aloud this time. "Have any of you seen her?"

"Not since we split up," replied Hamilton worriedly. "She was right behind me when we left the camp. Has anyone seen her?" No one had.

The phrase echoed in Ava's head. It had been her plan. If even one hippo was left behind, it would be her guilt as well. The hippos grew quiet as they settled in to wait for Heidi's return. Finally Avocado could wait no longer.

"She should have been here by now," she told them. "I'm going back to look for her."

"Let's all go look for her," said Harold Hippo,

surprising everyone.

"NO!" said Avocado quickly. "Thanks. But if we all went, we'd make so much noise that they'd find us in no time, even in the dark, and we'd all be rounded up again. No. I'd better go alone."

"You may need some help," said Herman calmly. "Can't cover much ground by yourself. Besides, we make a good team. I'll go with you."

She knew Herman was right. And if Heidi was in some kind of trouble, she might really need Herman again. She nodded in agreement. "Let's go then," she said. "The rest of you, take to the river so they can't track us. Head up the river to our rainy season grazing lands. If we run too late, we'll meet you there."

"I'm coming too," said Hamilton Hippo.

Surprise again! And Hamilton didn't sound so wimpy anymore. She knew he needed to help find Heidi. With no other comment, she simply said, "OK. Let's go!"

Ava's father started to say something, but he closed his mouth as quickly as he had opened it. Something was happening here that he didn't quite understand, and he was powerless to stop it. His little child...and the others too...were growing up right before his very eyes. He was so proud...and so sad all at the same time. He wanted to stop them...he wanted to go in their place, but he knew this was something they had to do. All he could manage was, "Be careful Avocado. We love you." What a hippopotamus she had become!

All the rest were quiet as they watched the three little hippos walk away. They had lost friends and loved ones to disease, sickness, predators, and other hunters before, but never had one of them been taken alive by this kind of hunter. It was a fate beyond their understanding, but somehow they knew it was something that none of them wanted to have happen.

As the three little hippos faded into the dark, it was Harold Hippo who spoke again. "We'd better go. They didn't set us free to be recaptured."

All but Ava's father and mother turned and began to walk away, silently and without speaking. Harris Hippo stood there staring at the darkness. "My little green Avocado..." he whispered to the night. "Be careful...and please come back to us." They lingered, staring into the black night a moment longer, then they too turned and headed up river.

Chapter Ten—The Rock

Ava, Herman and Hamilton were on their own now, and a more determined group you've never seen. They trotted steadily until they arrived back at the hunters' camp. The fire that had been only coals earlier was now a blazing bonfire. They heard the men talking and hollering back and forth across the compound.

"Didja find anything yet?" one hollered.

"Cawn't see a bloody thing in this dark," another replied. "Looks like they all got away!"

The one called Johnson muttered something to himself, and then hollered to all the other men. "Might as well come on in. We'll have to track them down in the morning. They can't get too far. Who woulda thought those blasted animals would be that smart?"

The little hippos looked at each other. They could see the cage door still hanging open just as they had left it. And there was no talk of having even one tiny hippo. "That means they haven't got her!" Ava told Herman excitedly. "But where is she then? She didn't make it back. She must be out there somewhere. She might be hurt or something. Let's split up and look for her."

"No," said Herman. "We need to stick together." Let's spread apart as far as we can and make circles around the camp. We just need to keep it quiet until we get farther away...and guys..." he added,

"Be careful."

She smiled at Herman and nodded. This was a side of him she hadn't seen before. He didn't seem at all like the hippo he was yesterday. But then, neither was she.

The young hippos started out about twenty feet apart, just far enough so they could still hear each other, but about a hundred yards outside of the camp. How will we ever find her...Avocado worried as she walked...without getting caught ourselves? She wasn't scared, but it seemed so hopeless in the vast darkness.

An hour passed, then two. They narrowed their search ring each time they circled the camp, each time getting closer and more in danger of being found out. It was Herman who finally said it.

"It's no use. We've looked everywhere. She must've gotten away from here. We'll just have to hope she catches up with us later. It's almost sunrise. We'll have to get out of here before the hunters get moving or we'll be the ones locked up."

"I know you're right Herman," said Hamilton. "We do need to be going. Let's just make one more round and then we'll go. I just hate to give up..." His voice tapered off into silence.

They finished one more time around the camp getting as close in as they dared. It was beginning to get light. "We've got to go now!" Herman said urgently. "The sun will be up soon and before long, the hunters will be after all of us. We've got to get as far away from here as we can!"

Ava and Hamilton took one more look around, straining their eyes to see anything at all in the dawning morning...but there was no Heidi. Together they sighed and turned their backs on the camp. As they walked away their heads swung from side to side...searching...never giving up. It was only a few minutes later that Ava stopped suddenly!

"What is it?" whispered Herman as he froze in his tracks.

In the shadows about thirty feet away, Ava thought she saw a movement. She felt panic thinking the hunters might have set a trap for them. She focused her eyes on the place, but all she could see were rocks and trees.

"Must have been a bird or something," said Herman.

"Maybe," said Ava, "but I won't feel right if we don't check it out."

Closer and closer they got to the source of the movement but there was nothing unusual. Then Hamilton saw it! He smiled inside at what he saw. One of the rocks appeared to have a tail! With another couple of steps, he was certain. It was a tail! And the "rock" was just about the right size to be...Heidi...or at least a part of Heidi. All that was visible of her was her rump. Avocado saw it too, smiled, and nudged Herman.

"Psst...look over there," she told him. Herman still didn't see what they were seeing. But that was all right with Ava. She knew it was Heidi! They had found her! As they drew closer still, Herman finally saw what Ava and Hamilton were smiling about.

"Heidi!" he shouted.

"Herman? Herman? Is that you?" a muffled voice asked. Heidi couldn't see her friends because she was wedged tightly between a tree and a boulder somewhat larger than her. She was indeed caught between...a rock and hard place.

"Yeh," said Herman. "It's me...and Ava and Hamilton too."

"Oh Heidi," said Avocado with a great sigh of relief. "I'm so glad we found you. We thought you might have been captured by the hunters...or you were hurt and helpless somewhere. We're so glad you're all right."

"Well," said Heidi. "I'm not exactly all right. And I'm trapped! I've been stuck here like this for hours! I'm sore! And my legs are cramping...I've been so miserable!" She began to sob. "I thought I'd never see any of you again...please help me get out of here," she cried.

She was caught all right. On her own, she would have been stuck here until her "Rock and a Hard Place Diet" helped her lose about 20 pounds for lack of food. Hippos are not fond of diets at all, but starvation diets are on the top of their list of nightmares. Though they were still not yet out of danger, the mood was much lighter now. Herman couldn't resist teasing Heidi just a little.

"How in the world did you ever manage to get yourself stuck like that?" he asked coyly...then he added, "but it is a very good disguise. From this angle, you look a lot like any other rock. I doubt they ever would have noticed you like that."

"Herman!" Ava scolded. "Quit fooling around and let's get her out of here! We're running out of time." But looking again at Heidi's tail, now wiggling frantically atop her rear end, she had to laugh, and so did Hamilton.

"Oh Heidi!" she giggled. "I'm so glad we found you!" Between the three of them, Herman and Hamilton pushing against the tree trunk, and Ava butting her head against Heidi's to force her out the way she came in, they were able to free her in seconds. And it was a good thing too. From the hunter's camp in the distance, they began to hear the sounds of truck engines starting. They looked at each other.

"Are you all right Heidi?" Ava asked. "We've really got to be going."

Though Heidi was a little stiff from her awkward position, she was happy to be free and ready to go. They were all thoroughly tired, but finding and freeing Heidi seemed to give them all a second wind. The long day and night were but a memory now.

They took off running. They ran...like the antelope...well, as much like antelope as four little stump legged hippopotami could. But they FELT like they were running like the antelope. Running wild and free...like children joyous and playful...even though their innocence was left behind them forever.

They had only gone a short distance when they heard sounds ahead. They looked at each other and without a spoken word, each knew what the other was thinking! THE HUNTERS! Quickly and very quietly, for hippos, they ducked into a nearby thicket. Breathlessly they waited. It was only in the quiet that Avocado seemed to recognize voices.

"...I only hope we're not too late," said one.

"We never should have let them go alone," said another. "What were we thinking?"

"We weren't thinking!" the other voice replied. "I guess..." But before he could finish his thought, Avocado jumped out from her hiding place.

"Dad!" she screamed happily. "I was beginning to think I'd never see you again."

"Thank goodness Avocado! You're all right! Where are the others?"

"Here we are!" exclaimed Heidi as she and Hamilton showed themselves.

"Me too!" chimed in Herman.

"Thank goodness!" repeated Harris Hippo. "I would never have forgiven myself if anything had happened to any of you."

"Hallelujah!" said the other hippo. It was only now that Avocado finally realized who the other hippo was. It was Harold Hippo. The old bigot himself! She grinned widely at him as he smiled at the young hippos. He continued. "You kids are more and more amazing all the time. I'm so proud of you all!" There were hippo hugs and hippo kisses all around...even for Harold...but then Ava reminded them it wasn't over yet.

"We've got to keep going," she said urgently. "The hunters were already moving by the time we found Heidi. It's only a matter of time before they'll be looking for us."

"Ava's right again as usual," said Harold Hippo with a tone of respect in his voice the like of which none had ever heard from him before. Only a few hours earlier he had seen nothing in Avocado except a small green useless aberration of a hippopotamus. Now his admiration shown through for all to see. "If we can get to the river," he said, "we'll be all right. Are you kids going to make it?" he asked worriedly seeing how worn they looked.

The four young hippos looked at each other and then up at the adults, smiling in unison. It was Herman who answered for all of them. "Yeh," he said, "I think we're all going to make it just fine now."

The events of the past day and night had lain hard upon the small band of hippos, but the joyous reunion and the unbelievable conversion of old Harold Hippo seemed to make it all feel like a brand new day. They all knew as Harold had said, that the river would indeed bring them safety. The river was wide and deep, and there was no place for humans to cross for miles...up or downstream. Though one might not think it from their appearance, hippopotami are excellent swimmers. And besides being able to swim well, they are able to stay under water for long periods of time because of their large lungs. They well deserve the nickname "river horse". They would be able to simply swim to safety on the other side, and the hunters would be left behind.

Chapter 11—Ring Around The...Avocado

The sun was already beginning to show over the treetops when the river came in to view. They had smelled the water for some time now, but it was only when they saw it that they slowed their pace. It seemed that now they were home free. Their steady trot slowed to a walk. But even as they began to catch their breath, Avocado's ears picked up an awful sound coming closer and closer. At first it was just a foreign sound. She knew it wasn't a usual jungle sound, but her senses, dulled by lack of sleep and exhaustion, couldn't quite make the connection...until suddenly it hit her! THE HUNTERS! That awful noise was their trucks! And from the increasing loudness she could tell they were only seconds behind them. The river was still fifty yards away. The trucks would be upon them before they could reach it!

"They're coming!" she shouted to the others. "RUN!"

But she knew it was no use. They'd never make it in time. She knew also that SHE had to do something. Suddenly she stopped...and turned to face the oncoming vehicles. When the hunters came into view, they were taken by surprise at little Avocado's standing still in front of them...and even more surprised...at her color! All of them stopped in their tracks when they saw her. Some of them were already standing poised on the backs of the trucks with nets that they had planned to throw over the hippos, but the little green hippo standing in their path brought all of them to a screeching halt!

"My gawd!" exclaimed Johnson. "Would you look at that? A green hippo..." He paused a moment in disbelief, and then with a new idea in his head, he began to bark out orders to his men. "Forget the rest of them mates," he hollered. "Let's get this one. It'll be worth more than all of the rest of them put together. Who would believe it? A green hippo!"

Herman heard the commotion and turned to see what was going on. His first impulse was to stay with Avocado, but he understood why she'd stopped...to give them a chance. He wanted to stay and help, but he knew he needed to keep the others moving. His voice choked as he urged them on, and he took one more look back before he too ran for the river barking urgent encouragement at the hippos in front of him.

Avocado stood her ground as the trucks entered the open area and the men began to surround her. From the sound of the splashing behind her, she knew the others had reached the river and were safe. Now she had to figure out how to save herself! If she was to escape, she had to wait for just the right moment to make her break. Though they could encircle her she figured they couldn't plug all the gaps effectively.

If she did it just right...NOW! She raced for a space between two of the hunters, one who she could see had his feet caught up in a net. It would be close...

She made it...just as the one hunter tripped and tangled himself in the net that was meant for her! She had escaped the circle...and there ahead of her...was the river!

She heard the man name Johnson shouting again and saying words she just didn't understand. The very last thing she heard was "Stop it! Shoot it if you have to! Even a dead green hippo will be worth something!" She heard guns firing, and what sounded like giant horseflys buzzing past her. She felt something hit her just as she reached the river's edge. She took a deep breath and prepared to dive...the deepest breath she had ever taken. Then she sank under the water...

Chapter 12---Ava Disappears

One by one the hippos pulled themselves from the water on the far side of the river and then ran into the cover of the bushes. They scarcely needed cover. The river was deep and wide at this point. The gunfire aimed at them from the other side was no real danger to them now. Even if they were hit by the bullets, at this distance they would only bounce off their tough hippo hides. The last of the hippos turned in time to see Avocado just now diving under the water. They were surprised to see her so far away. They all assumed she was right behind them. In the chaos, they hadn't seen that she had stayed behind to give them a chance to get away. It was only later that Herman told them what she had done.

The hippos stood watching. The insect like gunfire from across the river bothered them no more than tsetse flies. They watched the river now, expecting to see Avocado pop up at some point on her way across the river. Back and forth their heads bobbed, searching for an indication of where she might appear. Where was she?

The hunters on the opposite shore had quit firing now seeing that their efforts were hopeless. The man called Johnson stomped, kicked the dirt, and threw his hat on the ground...but that didn't help him. The rest of the hunters all focused their eyes on the river upstream and down, searching for a sign of the little green hippo.

"It hasn't come up yet," said one of them. "I know I hit it. Come on. Let's check downstream for the body. We've got to get something out of this."

The hunters abandoned their watch at the riverside and gathered again on their trucks. They headed downstream to look for the dead green hippo. They dreaded having to start all over again now that the hippo herd was lost to them. A green hippo hide was better than nothing.

On the other side of the river, the hippos also were still scanning the water for Ava. A little farther back away from the river, the rest of the pod had been waiting safely out of view. They now joined the smaller group at the river's edge. Herman explained to all of them what Ava had done.

"She should have come up by now," he stated simply at the end of his story.

"She should have come up by now."

Chapter 13---A Funeral March

The whole herd stood in silence watching the river. But, like Herman said, she should have come up by now. Five minutes passed without another word. Ten minutes. Then fifteen. As if any hippo could have stayed under that long without seeking more oxygen. They all knew it had been too long. No hippo could have stayed under that long...and lived.

No one wanted to speak. No one wanted to say it. They all wanted to be brave. They all wanted to have hope. But there was none to be had. It was Harold who finally spoke...with Avocado's words. "She said we should go upriver to our rainy season grazing land. She said we would be safe there..." he said. "We should go..."

At first no one moved. It was like they were all made of stone. Then, one by one, with Harold's gentle nudging, the hippos began to move. No more words were spoken as the group slowly departed from the riverside to follow the jungle trail. Finally, only five hippos remained. Hamilton and Heidi...and Harris and Hilda...and Herman.

They stood in stunned silence, unable to convince themselves to go on. Harris thought of his sweet little green hippo and all the joy she had given he and Hilda even though, and maybe especially because, she was different. He remembered her face through the bars of the hunters' cage, and the tone of voice that Harold had greeted her with. He thought then that they would never see her again. But now...after all they'd been through...it wasn't fair! "It's just not fair," he sobbed quietly to himself.

He remembered how she had taken it upon herself to go back to search for Heidi, alone if she had to. But most of all, he remembered the joy he felt when he and Harold found the four little hippos on the trail coming back from Heidi's rescue. He thought it was over then...that they would all go back to the others together and live happily ever after. He had not been prepared for this. The shock was so great that he wasn't sure if he could go on...but he knew Ava would have wanted him to...

As giant hippopotamus tears flooded his face.

And Hilda...poor Hilda. All she could see was the sad little face of Avocado when she tried to explain to her why the others didn't want to play with her. And now...she was gone. It wasn't fair. Hilda also broke down in tears. Together the two adult hippos mourned their great loss...while their tears formed a huge pool beneath them.

They might not have moved at all had it not been for Herman and Hamilton and Heidi. The three little hippos, each with their own hippo tears forming smaller pools at their own feet, couldn't speak...but together they nudged Ava's parents to follow the others. Together, they all stumbled along, unable to see but a blurry vision of a gray bobbing mass ahead of them.

It was like a funeral procession that day as they all plodded along. No one spoke about anything. Not about where they were going, how long it would take to get there, nor even about where they had been.

Nothing. It was as if they were all moving on autopilot, unknowing, uncaring, about anything...except Avocado's absence from their midst.

All of them, from the very eldest to the very youngest, understood what Avocado had done for the pod. And all of them were very much aware of how they had mistreated her. It only made the loss of her that much more painful for them. No chance even to say 'I'm sorry'. It was as if the world as they knew it...had ended that day.

The only sounds came from the leaves and twigs that crunched beneath their heavy hippo feet...and from the birds and monkeys going on about their business in the trees as if nothing had happened. The hippos saw and heard none of it. None of it mattered today.

Chapter 14---A Green Ghost

And none of them ever expected to see a green hippopotamus...

But there she was...just as green as you please...standing right there in front of them...and looking quite happy to see them.

"Hi there!" she said innocently. "What kept you?" She couldn't have known what they were thinking. They all looked at her in disbelief...as if they were seeing a mirage...or...or a ghost...

From the back of the group it was obvious that those in the front had stopped. The rhythm of the procession was interrupted, but Harris and Hilda didn't even notice as they came to a stop. It was only Heidi, the smallest hippo, who could see between the legs of the bigger adults...all the way through to the very strange vision in front of them. A strange GREEN vision. At first, she wasn't sure what to think. The color was so familiar, but her eyes were still blurred by tears. Could it be? She pushed her way to the front of the group...all the way up to the little green ghost hippopotamus...

"AVOCADO!" she shouted. "It IS you! Avocado, we thought you were dead! Where have you been?"

The others, who had not been quite sure what to believe, finally began to snap out of it. Everyone began talking at once. The last ones to even realize that something was going on were Harris and Hilda. They had been mourning so deeply that it was only the shouting and screaming that finally pulled them from their reverie. By then, a path had been cleared between Avocado and her parents. They couldn't believe their eyes. They had lost all hope that Avocado was alive. They didn't want to delude themselves, but they were sure they saw her right there in front of them!

By now, Avocado had heard enough to know what had happened. Why they were all so shocked, and why her parents held back. She wasn't about to let it go on a second longer.

"MOM! DAD! IT'S ME! I'M BACK! I MADE IT! I'M ALIVE!" She tried to make it as clear as possible for them. In her quieter voice she added. "We're all safe and alive," she said. She ran to greet them as they ran toward her.

When they met in the middle, there was such shouting and screaming that the whole jungle took notice! The birds and the monkeys in the trees stopped what they were doing. There was hippo hugging and hippo kissing, and even some hippo dancing! They hippo jumped, and bumped hippo rumps! Every hippo hugged and kissed every other hippo until they were all smothered and slobbered with huge happy hippo hugs and kisses! What had been a funeral march only minutes before was now the greatest hippo celebration of life that one could ever hope to see!

When they finally settled down enough to speak in a normal tone of voice, it was Harold Hippo himself who had something to say.

"Avocado," he began, through his own tears, "Avocado. We're all so glad that you're alive. It's hard to realize what truly stupid fools we've been. And me...I've been the biggest fool of all. I think I can speak for all of us when I say that we're so very sorry for the way we acted...especially me." He looked around at all the other hippos nodding their heads sheepishly.

"We can see now, that you're some special kind of hippo...and it has nothing to do with being green. We were wrong, and we were stupid to pick on you for being different from us. I only hope you can forgive us."

Avocado looked up at Harold, and then around at all the other hippos. She looked at her mother and father who were now crying tears of joy into another huge pool at their feet, and she remembered that she was not the only one to suffer from the teasing and being an outcast. Her parents grinned huge hippo grins at her through their tears. Their only thoughts now, were how happy they were to have her back from the "dead".

Besides, it was Avocado who had been the target of all their cruel jokes and taunts. It was little Ava who had to say now whatever there was that needed to be said. She looked once more around at the crowd whose all eyes were upon her...and then she spoke.

"Forgive what?" she asked. "If it's all right with all of you, I'd like to forget that it ever happened. How about it?"

The group was silent for a moment as if thinking

collectively about Avocado's words, and then...once again led by Harold... "All right!" he shouted. "Let's hear it for Avocado! HIP...HIPPO...HOORAY!" And they all gave her three big 'Hip-Hippo-Hooray' cheers!

It was only then that Harris Hippo noticed a gray line across the left side of Avocado's shoulder. "What's that?" he asked Avocado worriedly as the others also took notice of the gray line.

"I don't know for sure," Ava replied. "It felt like something bit me when I was running for the river."

"SHE'S BEEN SHOT!" gasped Harold Hippo. Every other hippo gasped as well and stared at Avocado as if she might collapse any moment.

Avocado shrugged her shoulders and winced a bit as the line went crooked with her shrug. "It only hurts a little," said Avocado. "And I'm all right now. I just want to go home...and relax."

All the other hippos, including Harris and Hilda, shook their heads in unison at Avocado's wound...not knowing what else to say or do. They were ready to go home too...so they all headed on up the river toward their grazing lands, chattering and visiting as if none of it had ever happened.

Chapter 15---The Final Chapter

And Avocado was never teased again. She grew up among the herd in peace and harmony. And when it came time, Avocado took Herman for her mate. They had several little hippos of their own...but none of them were green. And whenever the younger hippos of the pod would ask why Avocado was green, they were told the story of the day the hunters came...and how Avocado saved them all with her quick thinking and intelligence. But there was never a word mentioned about the way they had treated her before that day...nor about why or how she was green.

The truth is, no one ever figured out WHY Avocado was green. And of course, it never mattered anyway, except in the minds of a few thoughtless hippos who later learned that truth for themselves. And somehow, the little ones seemed to understand, and they never asked again why Avocado was green.

But they did ask...over and over and over...to be told the story of the day the hunters came. And, like good parents everywhere, the hippo moms and hippo pops told the story so many times that they could tell it in their sleep. And the little hippos cheered and cried their way thru the tale each time it was told. And at the end of every story, they all cheered three little 'Hip-Hippo-Hoorays' for Avocado...

And they all lived hippoly ever after.

THE END

Author's Note

I have recently reworked this book from an ebook to a paper print copy. In the meantime, I have added another title to my work. Among the other titles currently available either in ebook form or print or both, are "Santa Forgets", "Santa's Second String", "The Girl in the Window", and "Wishes".

If you read this, or any of my other tales, I would appreciate hearing what you think. You may reach me via email a charlesrhutson@gmail.com, or through my Facebook page. Or, if you really liked it, please write a review where you bought this book. Reviews give others a chance to know what you think as well...and maybe help me out at the same time.

Please keep an eye out as time goes on for other of my works at Amazon Books. Again, thanks for your consideration.

Made in the USA
Monee, IL
05 April 2025